LITTLE CRITTER'S®
THIS IS MY HOUSE

BY
MERCER MAYER

To Jace

A Golden Book • New York
Western Publishing Company, Inc., Racine, Wisconsin 53404

Western Publishing offers a wide range of fine juvenile and adult activities, games, and puzzles. For more information write Golden Press, 120 Brighton Road, Dept. M, Clifton, NJ 07012.

This is my house.
I live here.

My mom and dad
live here, too.

I have a dog.
I have a kitten.
They live in my house.

This is my little sister.
She lives here, too.

We eat in the kitchen.

We watch TV
in the family room.

Mom likes us
to play outside.

We have a swing.

We have a sandbox.

We have a tree house.

It is raining.
My little sister
should be inside now.

But the door
would not open, Mom.

We have stairs
in my house.

The stairs go to
our bedrooms.
I have my own room.

My little sister
has her own room, too.

I have a car.

I have an airplane.

I have paints.

Sometimes I play games
with my little sister.

Sometimes I let her win.

Sometimes we play
other games.

Sometimes Mom gets mad.

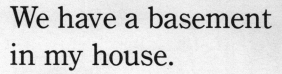

We have a basement
in my house.

Sometimes I have to
put my things
down here.

I love my house.
I love my mom and dad.

And...
I love my little sister, too.